BEYOND THE END

MOTHER MARY JOSEPH, O.C.D.

TRINITY COMMUNICATIONS
MANASSAS, VIRGINIA

ISBN 0-9347495-07-7

DEDICATION

*To our very dear friends
Br. Gerard and Maggie*

Table of Contents

Chapter I

No one paid any attention when an obscure astronomer sighted a new object in the sky and reported his find to the International Comet Center. The eyes of the world were on other matters. There had been two assassinations, three international financial scandals, and fourteen small wars were encircling the globe. Worst of all, the superpowers were each claiming to have developed a new and more destructive nuclear weapon, and the main question in everyone's mind was, "Who would be first to push the fatal button that would end everything?"

So the far away comet went unnoticed by the world until a junior astronomer at a large American observatory checked it as a matter of routine. His findings puzzled him.

"I don't think this is an ordinary comet," he said to the head astronomer.

The older man examined the observations and charts.

"You're right," he said tersely, annoyed at not being the discoverer. "It's something different. But what is it?"

The most sophisticated instruments were pointed at the distant object, then the head astronomer called the newspapers and triumphantly announced a new "find" in the universe. Since there had been a pause in the war alarms and scandals, the reporters were eager for news and flocked to the observatory.

"If this new object isn't a comet, what is it?" they asked, pad and pencil in hand.

"We don't know yet," answered the head astronomer. "It probably is a new type of star, but a most unusual one because its motion in space is irregular which, for the moment, makes it difficult for us to plot its path."

"Will it come close to the earth?"

"We don't know. As yet we don't have enough information to make any definite statement."

The newspapers had a field day asking everybody's opinion about this new stellar object, from astronomers with international reputations to the man on the street, until other events claimed the headlines; but just before this occurred, a young reporter facetiously named it the "Star Bomb".

When the head astronomer read that, he went white.

"I'm afraid they've hit on the right name," he murmured as the newspaper fell out of his shaking hands.

All the major observatories grew increasingly apprehensive although none dared to make a statement. Their knowledge, however, could not be kept secret for long, and as the news of their findings leaked out, the astronomers, one by one, reluctantly admitted that the "Star Bomb", as now all called it, was on a collision course with the earth.

No one knew where it came from—a Black Hole was a favorite theory—but all agreed that its inner core was surrounded by enormously hot gases whose heat would sear the earth before the collision. The facts were so conclusive that only the most blindly optimistic person could doubt them.

"NO HOPE," screamed one newspaper.

"THE END IS NEAR," trumpeted another.

Then in the eternal city of Rome, the Holy Father told the world of Heaven's latest warning. On the day the Star Bomb had been first sighted, he had been at his study window looking out over Rome as the great bells of St. Peter's were sounding the evening Angelus. In the sky he saw the Blessed Virgin standing with her arms held out and she was weeping. She looked at him and said, "The hour of God's justice has come. I can no longer hold back my Son's hand; He has been offended too often and too long. But this has been granted: the world my Son redeemed by His death will be saved from destroying itself. Men will be spared from committing that evil, and time will be given them to repent."

As the Star Bomb approached and men became convinced that their end was really near, several things happened. The wars faded away; officers and men saw no further reason for fighting and so went home. Getting rich became unimportant; what good was money for which there would be no use? Everywhere people slowly divided into two groups: those who believed in God and eternity, and those who did not. Houses of worship were crowded by the believers and the worst and wildest of amusement places by the others who attempted to obliterate their fears in loud and endless pleasures.

And the Star Bomb drew nearer and nearer. Its effects began to be felt. The polar ice caps melted; glaciers vanished; seas rose and engulfed shorelines. In the mountains huge avalanches broke loose and roared down the slopes, sweeping everything before them, leaving the rocky crags barren and stark against a pitiless sky. Streams disappeared, and then rivers and small lakes; fields and crops withered and burnt; leaves curled on the trees and dropped off. At first, those who could, fled to whatever place they thought would survive the longest, but at length everyone stopped running and waited for the end. Day by day more towns and cities perished until only a few places on earth had inhabitants. Finally the day came which all who still remained alive knew was their last.

One of these last places was a country town on the shores of Lake Michigan. When the discovery of the new stellar object had first been announced, before its threat to the Earth was known, few people in the town had paid much attention to it except for the freshman science class of St. Lawrence, the regional Catholic high school. The class had become so interested that it had a special project on comets and other stellar curiosities.

"I'm almost fed up with comets, quasars, black holes and such, Aunt Mattie," said Celia Moreland when she came back one afternoon to the old fashioned white shingle house on the shady side street where she lived with her great-aunt. "Tomorrow we'll dismantle the project and look around for something new. I wonder what we'll do next?" she continued as she tossed her books onto a chair and took the makings of a sandwich out of the refrigerator.

Aunt Mattie laughed. "I think I can tell you what it will be—getting the school ready for a visit from a Cardinal."

"A Cardinal!" Celia yelped in excitement. "Are you joking, Aunt Mattie?"

"No, indeed, Cardinal Antonio is coming here. He's an old friend of Father Bruno from the days when they studied together in Rome. The Cardinal is on some sort of world wide mission for the Pope, and when he comes to this country he plans to spend a few days with Father. Father himself told me and said that he was going to ask the Cardinal to give a talk at St. Lawrence High. So getting ready for the Cardinal's visit will probably be your next project."

"A talk on what?"

"I have no idea."

"Probably on religious vocations," said Celia gloomily. "They all talk on that. Oh, I know that priests and sisters are desperately needed, but another topic would really make us listen."

Cardinal Antonio did not talk on vocations.

"It was odd," Celia reported to her aunt. "He spoke as though he thought time was running out for everyone, and said that we must try to crowd into our lives as much love of God and our fellow man as we could and to pray fervently to the

Blessed Mother. Sounded a little weird."

One evening their pastor, Father Bruno, brought the Cardinal over to dinner.

"Here," said Father Bruno, as he introduced Celia's aunt, "is a person who loves the Mass as much as any priest I have ever known, and she spreads this love around her."

"It's a tradition in our family," Celia's aunt explained. "We are descended from Margaret Clitherow, the Yorkshire housewife, who was pressed to death under heavy doors in the Elizabethan persecution because she concealed priests and had Mass said in her home."

During the meal the Cardinal was so friendly that Celia revised her opinion of him. He wasn't weird but very nice, only she wished that he would show more interest in her desire to study music after finishing high school.

"I want to help spread good religious music," said Celia eagerly, hoping this would get a response. "I only wish I could think of a different way to do it—something that would really catch people's attention."

"Celia will find a different way," said the old pastor to the Cardinal. "She has a streak of . . . well, shall we call it determination ."

Celia laughed. "Stubbornness, Father, go on and say it."

Cardinal Antonio smiled at her. "Stubbornness in God's cause has made many saints. The trouble is that we often convince ourselves that what we want is God's will for us."

"Wishful thinking is what we call it. It's a normal human disease. I know the effects only too well," said the pastor ruefully.

"So do I," said Aunt Mattie, and the meal ended with laughter.

As the Cardinal left he blessed the house saying—Celia noticed a deep sadness in his voice—"This is truly an island of faith in a world that is growing more and more pagan. But there are fewer and fewer such islands, and then . . . ," he left the sentence unfinished.

When he and Father Bruno had gone, Celia said to her aunt, "See what I told you. He sounds as though he thought the world was coming to an end."

"Perhaps he is right," answered her aunt quietly.

Not long after the Cardinal had returned to Italy, the full news of the Star Bomb hit the world. In the beginning many in the small Michigan town dismissed it as a piece of alarmist reporting thought up by the big city papers who had nothing better to do. Father Bruno and Aunt Mattie, however, believed it immediately.

"The Cardinal knew," she said to her great-niece. "The Holy Father must have told him about the vision of Our Lady over Rome before making it public. The Cardinal wanted to prepare you; that's why he gave you that talk."

The old pastor was a pillar of strength to the solidly Catholic farming community. "Pray, pray," he urged them. "Do penance and keep close to Jesus and His Mother, and above all pray the Mass with all your hearts. *There* is all our hope and power. Who knows but that God may once again have mercy on us and spare us this destruction, and if He does not, then let us thank Him for giving us time to prepare our souls to meet Him."

If the white haired priest gave strength to his flock, Aunt Mattie also brought comfort and peace to those who came to her for support.

It's probably easier for her since she is old (Aunt Mattie was seventy), decided Celia who went in turn from despair to rebellion, to a real determination to accept God's will. "It must be your will, Jesus," she said one day during Mass, "but it's so hard, I wanted to do so much for You." Every evening at their garden shrine of Our Lady of Fatima, she recited the rosary with her aunt and neighbors for the world that they now knew was really passing away forever. In between these times of prayer came the rebellion.

During one of these periods Celia came home one day and found Aunt Mattie at her big floor loom weaving a table runner that she had started before the future had been turned upside down by the Star Bomb.

"Aunt Mattie," she burst out impatiently. "How can you bother to work on that. What use will it be?"

"I would like to finish it, dear, if there is time. I hate to leave things undone."

"What does it matter if you finish it or not? What does anything matter anymore," Celia asked despairingly. But when the heat and parched air had made her aunt too feeble to weave, she herself finished the last six inches and caught the ends in decorative tassels. She tried to be cheerful about it for her beloved aunt's sake, but as she cut the warp from the loom she felt as though she were cutting all the threads of her life. Also to please Aunt Mattie Celia carefully tended her aunt's favorite house plants, two valiant coral geraniums; the other plants had given up.

Then came the time when the earth was down to its final hours and only a few persons were left in the town. Father Bruno celebrated his last Mass in the parish church of St. Peter's and then exposed the Blessed Sacrament on the altar, saying, "Let us spend our last moments here adoring Him whom we shall adore for all eternity."

Celia, who was among the handful of people present, reluctantly stood up and stepped out of the pew. She would have liked to stay with the remaining worshippers.

"Don't go," whispered a friend beside her.

"Aunt Mattie's alone and I . . . ," her voice trailed off.

Aunt Mattie, too feeble, for once, to attend the Mass she so loved, had said, "Go for us both." No, Celia could not leave her alone in these last hours, besides she longed for the comfort of her aunt's calm strength and unwavering faith.

She went out past the statue of her old friend, St. Anthony and his stand of burnt-out vigil lights, into the street. Dusk should have fallen, but instead of the refreshing, deepening gray of twilight, the sky was a lurid yellow-green; the air was scorching and left a bitter taste in her mouth. She held a handkerchief to her face, then dropped it. What was the use? What did an hour more or less matter? Her head was aching as she went down the deserted street under bare, dead trees where only a few twisted leaves remained clinging to the withered branches, past St. Lawrence High School. She had so looked forward to her second year there. Now the empty building seemed a symbol of all her vanished hopes and dreams for the future.

Through the open door of a small bar came the sound of a popular tune played by a battery operated recorder. As Celia passed, it stopped, and then the tune began again. The place was deserted. How long had the machine been playing the same thing over and over . . . how long would it go on after no one was left to hear it? She shuddered, tried to hurry and found she was staggering. Why hadn't she stayed in church? She would never make it home. She caught hold of a tree to keep from falling and managed to go on. Stumbling, she made her way to her aunt's house, half crawled up the steps, opened the door, and slid in quickly shutting it behind her. Here at last she could breathe though the air was stale and the terrible acrid odor was creeping through the tightly closed windows.

Aunt Mattie was where Celia had left her, in a comfortable chair in front of the little nook that held a shrine, her prayer corner, she called it. Her eyes were shut but her hands were very slowly letting a rosary slip through her old fingers. Celia bent down and kissed her aunt gently, then, overcome with exhaustion, dropped onto the couch and closed her eyes. She tried to think, to pray, but exploding volcanoes and rains of fire seemed to be in her brain. Opening her eyes, she reached for a tightly closed bottle of orange juice which was on the table beside her, unscrewed the top and drank from it. She could no longer taste anything but the liquid eased her parched throat for a few moments. With a great effort she pulled herself to her feet and went over to Aunt Mattie. There was no movement; the rosary hung loosely in the stiffening hands, and the lined face shone with an expression of ultimate peace.

For a moment Celia stood looking at her aunt, then in growing horror at the drooping geraniums, and at the rose pink wallpaper which had become a hideous color in the yellow-green light. The empty house was eerily silent. Unable to stand it any longer, she ran to the door. She would go back to St. Peter's. People must be there; she couldn't be the last person alive. As she opened the door a searing blast of heat hit her. She fought against it and managed to get down the steps but could not go on. She knew she couldn't make it to the church and swayed, desperately trying to focus her mind. No thoughts, no prayers came. Nothing. Blindly she turned towards the garden shrine where the Immaculate Mother looked down on the little shepherds of Fatima, took one step then fell forward into utter blackness.

Chapter II

Blackness. Yet just as it completely enveloped her, she felt as though something had caught hold of her and cool air brushed her scorched face. The blackness was like a river that was sweeping her along, swirling around and even through her. But the coolness continued also, and gradually she felt herself coming up, up through the darkness which was turning gray. A cool breeze *was* blowing over her so refreshingly that she did not want to open her eyes for fear it would stop. It was such a relief from the parched, acrid air of the final days of earth!

At last she did open her eyes but could not believe what she saw and closed them again afraid that she was having hallucinations. After a few moments, she opened them once more. No, it was true. She was lying on a low bed in a room with cream colored walls. Turning her head in the direction of the breeze she saw a window through which she glimpsed far-off mountains, then she looked around the room. On the opposite wall was a hanging whose pattern had a graceful upward sweep. The rest of the walls were plain, and the entrance was covered with another hanging. There was a table, a wooden chest against one wall and a wooden stool. Celia turned back to the window and lifted herself on one elbow in order to see farther out.

"How are you feeling, my dear daughter?" The voice was

richer and more musical than any she had ever heard. Celia dropped back onto the bed and stared at the figure that had come into the room and was standing beside her. It was tall, nearly six feet, and looked like a human being except that its eyes were larger than human eyes, or appeared to be, because the deep lavender-blue iris were so big that little white showed. They were beautiful eyes; beautiful and kind, set in a gentle and serene face that was framed by glorious golden brown hair caught in two long tresses.

"Am I dead?" Celia whispered.

"No, my daughter. You were brought here when your world ended and I am Dara, your new mother." The woman turned and called, again in that wonderfully rich voice, "Tormin, our new daughter is awake." With that she bent over and kissed Celia first on the forehead and then on each cheek. As she straightened up, another taller figure entered the room.

"Here is your father," said the woman, smiling. Before Celia could do or say anything, the man leaned down and kissed her in the same way, on the forehead and then on each cheek. As he did so she saw that his eyes were also very large, gray flecked with gold, and his straight dark brown hair came nearly to his shoulders.

Celia had been too bewildered to feel anything except surprise, but now she sat up looking fearfully from one to the other. Both were dressed in beige tunics that came to the knee, a broad stripe ran from each shoulder to the hem; rose stripes on the woman and green on the man. Each had a leather belt with a knife hanging in a sheath from it.

"Who--who--are you? Where am I? How did I get here? Please—tell me," Celia stammered, terrified.

The woman knelt beside the bed and put an arm around her. "Poor child, do not fear, you are safe."

The man said, in a voice as musical though deeper than his wife's, "You did not know you were coming here?" He sounded surprised.

Celia stared open-mouthed. "Know I was coming here! I don't even know where *here* is. All I know is that the earth was going to be blown to bits by the Star Bomb and I was suffocating and burning up, and there was such a terrible blackness. Then just at the end there came a slight coolness and I felt someone catch me."

"I caught you, my daughter," said the man, "just before your world perished."

"We were waiting for you," continued the woman. "And then we were given a sight of the terrible end of your world. In those last moments your father took you in his arms and we were brought back here, to Koinia[1], which is our world."

Celia's head was whirling. "But how did you know I was coming?"

"The Lord God told us," said Tormin. "And we rejoiced greatly that He was giving us a child, for we have none."

"Blessed is He," added the woman. Their faces were alight as they said these words and through the mists that were still swirling in her mind Celia remembered Aunt Mattie's last luminous expression.

Tormin continued. "The Lord God told us that your world had become so evil from disobedience to His commandments and from rejection of His love that it was going to be destroyed, cast out of the universe. Yet, for the sake of His Son's sacrifice for your world—what it was the Lord God did not tell us—He would take children from some of your families who still served Him, and would give them to those of us who had no children, for us to love and train in His ways . . . and with them would come great gifts."

Since Celia was still staring utterly dumbfounded, he asked, "Did not the Lord God ever speak to any in your world?"

"Yes, oh, yes, he did. It's in the Bible . . ." And with that the old figures of the Bible came alive for her as they had

---

[1]Pronounced Ko-ée-nee-ah

never done before, and she understood that those great men and women, Moses, Deborah, Elijah, had indeed talked with God . . . and if they, then why not others, why not these people? "But where in the universe are we? How did you bring me here?"

"Koinia is far from where your world was, far even for light that travels so fast." (So they know about the speed of light thought Celia in surprise.) "And I do not know how we were taken to your world and brought back."

"You don't know! Didn't you have some sort of spaceship? You must have had something."

The woman put her hand gently on Celia's lips. "Hush, child, do you need to know everything? Is it not enough to know that it is the Lord God's will, and what He wills is done without need of us or our little knowledge?"

"We always want to know the how and why of everything. That's supposed to show intelligence," protested Celia.

"And your world has perished. The Lord God did not need its intelligence," said Tormin. There was a severity in his voice that made Celia hastily change the subject.

"Yes, we were in a horrible mess, one we had made ourselves though we were warned and warned." Lourdes, Fatima, the Popes, yes there had been many warnings. "And how you could possibly want as a daughter someone from my earth is more than I can see." Celia thought resentfully, I suppose they were waiting for me like a dose of medicine God said they should take. She glanced up at them almost sullenly. They were looking down at her with eyes full of love, and for an instant as though through a rift she glimpsed a love too vast for even their minds and knew that the love they were offering her was a true part of that other and infinitely greater love. Her whole being cried out for this love, but then the moment was gone and left her feeling as though she were deep down struggling towards something she wanted desperately. She felt lonely and lost.

"What shall I call you?" she asked timidly. Even as she

asked she felt a small surge of independence. They certainly appeared to be extremely kind but she did not want to call two strangers from another world, no matter how good, father and mother . . . at least right off.

"Since you do not want to call us father and mother," said the woman, and there was sadness in her voice. Celia flushed and dropped her eyes . . . how had the woman known she did not want to? "Then call us Tormin father and Dara mother until your heart tells you differently."

"I had a mother and father," Celia said defensively because her conscience reminded her that she could barely remember her dead parents. Kind old Aunt Mattie had been her whole family. The couple said nothing for a moment, then her new father asked, "What is your name, my daughter?"

"Celia, for St. Cecilia."

"That name has music in it," he said. "I think you have music in you as well."

"St. Cecilia is the patroness of musicians. I love music and singing, too." Celia was very proud of her voice, a contralto, the St. Lawrence Glee Club director had said.

"That is good," said her new mother, Dara, "for our world is full of music. But come."

They led her into the kitchen, a large, bright room with a brick oven, a fireplace, and shelves full of colorful pottery plates, bowls and mugs. A fire was smoldering, and half buried in the hot ashes was a cooking pot. The cheerful homeyness of the room revived Celia's spirits a little. She had deplored the endless number of kitchen gadgets of earth and had been glad that Aunt Mattie had few of them, but here she remembered them with some regret. These people must be very primitive, she decided, though when she glanced at the furniture, a large table, a smaller one against a wall, and several stools, she was surprised to find them really handsome.

"You must be very thirsty from the heat of those last hours," said Tormin, taking a two-handled mug from a shelf. He filled it from a tall, narrow container, also of pottery, and handed it to Celia. She took it gratefully and was about to drink when a shaft of suspicion went through her like a knife. What was in it? What were they trying to do to her? Perhaps they were angry because she did not want to call them father and mother. She hesitated, then remembered their look of love and the greater love she had seen behind theirs and determinedly drank. Long afterwards she understood that in that one act of trust she had taken a great step into the spirit of her new world, a spirit where the faintest shadow of suspicion was unknown.

Belatedly, Celia remembered her manners. "Thank you so much, Tormin father and Dara mother. You were so good to take me in sight unseen. I'm truly grateful and I'll try to do the best I can." Then curiosity got the best of her. "Please may I ask a few questions?"

The couple laughed. "Certainly, all you wish, dear daughter," said Dara. "But you must also learn what questions not to ask because asking them would be a lack of trust in the Lord God."

A trust that never wavered, a perfect trust, she had another fleeting glimpse, but this time of what earth's humans had lost in the fall.

While speaking, Dara had lifted the pot from the hot ashes, and Tormin had taken plates and bowls from the shelves.

"Come," he said, "we will have our evening meal."

Celia followed Dara and Tormin onto a small terrace of flat stones and caught her breath at the view. The house was perched on the bank near the end of a huge lake whose deep blue water was alive with ripples in the early evening breeze. To the right the shore stretched out of sight in an undulating line while to the left it curved until it was directly opposite them, then it curved back out of sight and reappeared as a distant indistinct line of green that faded into a horizon of darkening water.

Here and there Celia could see houses, and what looked

like carefully tended fields, in cleared spaces, but most of the slopes were thickly wooded. Trees, what trees! There were great giants of the forest with trunks eight and ten feet in diameter with deep green or reddish arching heads: tall slim trees with white trunks and rose-gray leaves that soared above the others like watch-towers over a swaying domain. And the flowers! They were all shapes and sizes, while their multi-hued colors were like those of the magic rainbows in Celia's old fairy tales.

What struck her the most was the silence. No planes, no motors nearby or on far off highways or distant fields. Just silence, a silence which was intensified rather than broken by the whish of the breeze and the late song of a few birds which seemed woven into the silence rather than distinct from it.

"How beautiful. Earth must have once been like this. Why did we have to lose it?" Celia said aloud.

"You had beauty like this and lost it?" said Tormin. "Sit down, child, and tell us about it." He and Dara had arranged the supper on a wooden table and drawn up benches. Celia sat down promptly. The sight of the food made her realize how hungry she was.

"Adam and Eve caused all our trouble," she began sadly, and told them the story of the Fall and the loss of the garden of Eden.

"It was the same with us," said Tormin. "We, too, were put to a test long ago."

"What happened? What was it like?"

"That I may not tell you, but the test was given to many, not only to two as in your world." He smiled at her astonished expression. "Must the Lord God act the same way in every world? Yes, many were put to the test. Some were faithful and others were not. They, like Adam and Eve, would not obey. At that time all the Koinians lived together many days' journey distant from here, but after the disobedience they separated for their thoughts and ways were no longer the same. Those who had obeyed lived in a valley on one side of a large mountain and the others, Thabons they called themselves—they would no longer bear our name—lived on the other side in another valley. Not long after the trial a great explosion came from the mountain between them, and it rained fire and rocks and death."

"A volcano!" Celia cried. "We have them also."

"The two groups were driven far. The Thabons in one direction and the Koinians who were our forefathers, in another. Both lost many in the flight."

"Both those who failed and those who did not?" exclaimed Celia. "That doesn't seem fair." She subsided quickly as she saw a warning look on Tormin's face. "Uh, please go on."

Tormin continued. "Not many of the Koinians were left, and of those some could no longer bear children." Radiation, thought Celia. "Now we are again increasing, but not the Thabons. If any of them remain, they must be very few and soon will be gone. For that was their punishment, to decrease until there were none left.

"Your first parents repented, you say. The Thabons did not. Even when they knew their punishment, they still would not repent, but went from evil to evil. Now they who were once our brothers hate us."

"Hate you!"

"Yes, because we did not fail the test, and though we diminished in numbers, we lost nothing in mind and heart. Rather where they turned from the Lord God, we have drawn even closer."

Celia nodded sorrowfully. "The same evil happened to us. In the end there were many, very, very many who not only denied God . . . the Lord God . . . but also hated and persecuted and even killed those who were faithful to Him."

The evening meal was over, and the sun was disappearing behind the mountains in a blaze of deep rose and pinks. All three had fallen silent. Tormin and his wife appeared to be listening to something, but Celia heard nothing except the usual twilight noises of trees and animals.

"Do you hear something?" she asked after waiting a few minutes.

"Can you not hear the music, my daughter," said Dara. "It is all around us."

"Music?"

"Music of the stars, the winds, the trees, of all creation."

Celia shook her head. Night was rapidly falling, and the growing darkness made her feel terribly lonely in this strange new land, and she longed desperately for her own earth. At least she could sing and in this manner, perhaps, join in the music she could not hear. Singing always lifted her spirits. She hoped that these Koinians would like her voice and think it as promising as her music teacher had.

"Do you sing?" she asked politely. "I love to sing."

"So do we. We shall teach you our songs and you will teach us yours," said Dara.

Hand in hand she and her husband stood on the edge of the terrace looking out over the lake and began to sing. Celia was enthralled. Never had she heard such voices, so rich and clear, so full of unfathomable depths. Melody and harmony were perfectly blended. The sound lifted her spirits and she was so lost in the music that, for a while, she did not listen to the words. When she became conscious of them, she gathered that it was a hymn of thanksgiving: for the creation of the universe, for their world, for all the beauty and goodness that was poured out on them and every theme ended with, "Blessed be the Lord God . . . Blessed is He." As the song finished with a thanksgiving for the coming night with its peace and sleep, Celia found herself joining in the refrain, "Blessed be the Lord God . . . Blessed is He."

"Now you sing for us, my new daughter," said Dara. "We would like to hear a hymn from your world."

After hearing them Celia did not want to sing, what was her voice, or any voice on earth, as compared with theirs?

Tommy had been right. Way back in second grade Tommy, the son of a music teacher, had been asked to explain original sin, and he had answered: "We struck God's piano all wrong and were never able to get back in tune again." Had earth been a silence in God's harmony as she had read somewhere, or had it been a discord? Probably a discord, and her voice would be full of it. But there was nothing else to do except sing. They were waiting and sooner or later they would have to hear her voice, so it might as well be now.

She looked across the almost dark lake to the opposite shore where the fading light had turned the mountains into black silhouettes. Above the tree tops hung a huge bright star. As she watched it grow more radiant as the sky darkened, she forgot about Dara and Tormin and the effect she hoped to produce with her voice and sang,

Hail, Queen of Heaven, the Ocean Star,
Guide of the wanderer here below,
Thrown on life's surge, we claim thy care,
Save us from peril and from woe,
Mother of Christ, Star of the Sea,
Pray for the wanderer, pray for me.

She ended the last verse, "Pray for thy children, pray for me," in tears and her heart cried out, "Blessed Mother, O Blessed Mother, you do know I'm here, don't you? And you'll still look after me, won't you? They may not need you, but I do."

Brushing the tears from her face she turned around wondering what they would say. The faces of the couple had been beautiful when they sang, but now they were radiant, and again, they seemed to be listening to something.

After a long while Tormin spoke. "Who is this Queen? Tell us, for your song was full of the music of heaven and the spirits of Light were listening."

Celia was startled, but, of course, if these Koinians had always been faithful and never done wrong, they had not needed a Redeemer, and so no Jesus, no Blessed Mother. And she felt sorry for this world, beautiful though it was.

"I'll try," she said. She told them of the Lord God's promise to the repentant Adam and Eve, which had been fulfilled in Jesus, the Son of God become man, and in Mary, His Mother. She was afraid of their reaction to the terrible events of Jesus' Passion and Death, but she did not get farther than Bethlehem.

"Mary, the Lady Mother, chosen by the Lord God—ah, what a mother she must be," Dara said this like a prayer.

"The mother above all mothers . . . and come from a fallen world," Tormin said in a tone of wonder and amazement.

"Yes, she is our Mother and she warned us. How she tried to warn us." Celia told them about the warnings Our Lady had given the world during her apparitions at Lourdes and at Fatima, and how the warnings had gone unheeded.

"Of course a mother would warn her children and do all in her power to save them," said Dara. "Ah, dear daughter, what a gift you have brought us. Now teach us your song."

Celia had only to recite it once and they knew it immediately. Then together the three sang the praise of the Mother of God in a world that had not known her.

Chapter III

The sky outside her window was bright when she woke up for the second time in her new world, and the far off mountains were sharply clear in the early morning sunlight, a sunlight that was definitely rosy in hue. Celia yawned and sat up in bed as the memory of yesterday flooded back. She again looked around the room studying it carefully which she had been too tired to do the evening before when her . . . her . . . new mother—how strange that word sounded even in her thoughts—had helped her go to bed and then kissed her with the three kisses. The feel of them had lingered through the night. Perhaps they were some sort of liturgical symbol. Celia hooked her arms around her knees and sat thinking. Yesterday she had been on the dying earth, a barren and scorched planet, and herself near death. Today she was on Koinia, a place vibrant with life, peace and music, in another part of the universe, perhaps in a different galaxy, and she wasn't supposed to ask why. She grinned to herself ruefully. Father Bruno had always said, "Celia, my child, you want to do God's will, but you also want to know His reasons. Never ask Him why. Just let Him do as He pleases." Evidently this point was going to be enforced here. She would have to learn to conform with everything, and deep down inside her a bit of rebellion again raised its head. Of course, she was glad to be in this world and very grateful to God for bringing her here, and she very much wanted to do His will, but surely that didn't mean she had to conform in everything; she would like to keep a little of her own identity, the identity of Celia Moreland from Michigan, in the great U.S.A..

Celia decided she had better get her thoughts straightened out before seeing them—must practice calling them Tormin father and Dara mother, she reminded herself. They were so . . . she searched for the right word, could not find it, and let her mind go off on another track. How beautiful last night had been after the terrifying and suffocating death agony of the earth. Aunt Mattie and Father Bruno would have loved Dara and Tormin's instant appreciation and reverence for Our Lady. It was as though they had fathomed and acknowledged Mary's greatness with one sweep of their minds. Celia hugged her knees disconsolately, suspecting that in that instant they had understood more than she with all her years of religion classes. How was she, an ordinary human being, and a fallen one at that, ever going to fit in here?

The room was growing brighter, and a delicious odor of something cooking made her realize how ready she was for breakfast. At least she didn't think there was anything to fear in this land of Koinia, and her spirits rose optimistically as she slid out of bed.

After saying her morning prayers—she would have to revise them to fit her new needs in this different world—she put on the tunic and sandals that were on the stool by her bed. The night before Dara had taken them from an old chest, saying, "These were once mine when I was a child. Tomorrow I will start weaving you a new tunic and your father will make you new sandals."

The leather belt had a sheath with a knife in it like Dara's and Tormin's. She drew the knife out gingerly. It had a broad, short blade with very sharp edges and a blunt, slightly pointed end, nothing at all like her Girl Scout knife.

As she went out of the room, she stopped to examine the hanging that served as a door—the only real doors were the exterior ones. Like the tunics, it was handwoven, but, unlike them it had a pattern worked in several colors that looked deceptively simple, but Celia knew that only an expert could have woven it. Strange, though, that the tunics were plain while the hangings were so beautiful. Two more hangings, intricate ones, were in the next room which also had plain walls. As she looked at the furniture, she revised her opinion of the night before; these Koinians were definitely not primitive. It was simple, yes, but perfectly made. The wood of the chairs had been cut and polished so that the strange wavy grain showed to its best advantage, while around the edge of the table was one line of magnificent carving that was highlighted by the straight grained wood. How often she had seen the beauty of materials lost under over-ornamentation. Now she understood, the plainess of the walls focused the eye at once on the graceful and colorful hangings. This thought almost reconciled her to the loss of the multi-colored wallpapers of which she had been so fond. The clink of pots reminded her of breakfast and she hurried into the kitchen where Dara greeted her with the three kisses. Celia asked if these three kisses had a special meaning.

"This is how we greet or take leave of those very dear to us. It is a sign of the two persons' mutual love of God, love of each other, and their thanksgiving for these loves."

"How beautiful," said Celia as she returned them. Earth's greetings had lacked depth in comparison.

Breakfast had turned out to be as delicious as it smelt. While she ate, she watched Dara moving gracefully about the room.

"Dara mother, why do you wear clothes?"

Dara looked up tranquilly. "Why? Did you not wear clothes in your world? The Lord God did not give us fur or feathers to protect us as He gave to the animals, but instead He gave us the knowledge to make what we need." She laughed. Celia already loved that laugh, it was so gentle and merry. "How you children would be scratched by the bushes and stones when you run and play if we did not make you tunics and sandals."

Celia propped her elbows on the table and dropped her chin in her hands. "Yes, we wear . . . wore . . . clothes, but with us it was the result of original sin. Adam and Eve did not know they were naked until after they had disobeyed God."

"They did not know they were naked?" Dara was puzzled. She turned to her husband who had just come in. "I do not understand. Do you, Tormin?"

"No. Was it wrong on your Earth not to wear clothes," he questioned.

They had considerable difficulty in understanding how warped the minds of the inhabitants of Earth had become in regard to the human body.

Dara shook her head. "From what evils we have been kept by the faithfulness of those who came before us. We wear clothes because we need them and when we need them, not because our eyes and our minds have become twisted."

"Our minds were twisted in many ways. Yesterday you said others were brought here from Earth besides me. We all have original sin, and I'm afraid we'll bring trouble down on you," said Celia worriedly. The possibility of being responsible for pulling down this unfallen world was most unpleasant.

Tormin shook his head gravely. "You will not be permitted to. Remember that, my new daughter. A special strength will be given you, but you will still be able to choose. Choose rightly and come to us for help and counsel when you need them. It will only be in the beginning that you may have difficulty seeing clearly. In the end, though you will never be fully like us, you will be able to come close to us in mind and heart, and when you have children, they will be born free of all shadow as ours are. But be very faithful."

"I will try hard," she promised wondering what he meant

by "special strength".

Most of the morning she spent watching Tormin making pottery. She tried her hand at shaping a bowl on his foot driven potter's wheel and had a good laugh at her lopsided result.

"Do all of the Koinians make pottery or do the others buy them from you?" she asked.

"Buy? What does that word mean?"

Celia tried again. "Do you sell these things? I mean do the other Koinians pay you for making pottery for them?"

Again Tormin did not understand. "What is sell and pay?"

When he finally understood what *buy*, *sell* and *pay* meant, Tormin frowned. "No, I make these things because that is a gift the Lord God has given me, and a gift is to be shared with others. Those who need what I can make come to me or to another one who does the same work, and I go to those who have other gifts for my needs."

He told her that some work all did, such as weaving, but the really beautiful pieces were done by those who had that special gift. Dara was one of them. "It is music to watch her weave," he said. "She will teach you. As time goes by we shall see what gifts are yours."

"I don't think I have any," Celia was very dubious. Singing had been her only accomplishment.

"Everyone has special gifts. Is not working in the fields and making things grow a gift? Is not caring for a home and children a special gift? Is not being a husband or wife, a father or mother, a special gift?"

"I'm afraid not many in my world thought of gifts in that way. Long ago, I think they did, but in my time a gift was something that made a person more important in some way or another and usually brought them more money." She went dismally on, "I'm afraid you're going to find out that I just don't fit in here very well."

Tormin laughed at that remark. "The Lord God does not make mistakes. But you must try."

"Will I be allowed to choose what I want to do?"

"Certainly. Each must decide for themselves what is their gift. We will help you as much as we can, but the decision must be yours."

This sounded too good to be true; to be able to choose freely what one wanted to do without having to struggle against competition or opposition or even envy—she was sure there was no such thing as envy here—what a wonderful world this was. Then she became dismal again.

"But suppose I decide to develop a wrong gift?"

"There are no wrong gifts, only the wrong use of them. The Thabons were given the same gifts as we were, but they used them to harm and for their own selfish purposes. They forgot that, as I said, gifts are to be shared."

"I'm afraid a great many people on earth used their gifts only for themselves."

"They must have been very lonely," was Tormin's surprising comment. He took another piece of clay and Celia watched, fascinated, as he shaped it on his wheel into a graceful jar, singing softly as he did so.

"I think your song is going into that jar!" she exclaimed. "Its tones were deep and sustained when you formed the broad lower part, then they were higher and faster as you sloped inward and upward, and they lilted when you made the neck, and you ended with a gay measure as you turned the lip."

Tormin smiled at her amazement. "Of course. All work should be music."

"And so every piece you make will hold music in it until it breaks . . . how glorious!" cried Celia. She looked at the row of already shaped pottery that was waiting to be fired; now she could see a song in each one of them. "And what of the song itself? Will it go out into space?"

"Yes, indeed."

Celia threw back her head and clapped her hands with delight. "Oh, I can see the shape of that jar in music soaring upwards forever and ever."

She laughed at the picture and Tormin laughed with her. Celia liked his laugh also though it was very different from Dara's.

"I love yours and Dara mother's laugh," she burst out spontaneously. "It's so real. I don't think I ever heard such real laughter before. There's nothing in it but laughter."

That was it. All the laughter she had heard on earth had something mixed in it: ridicule, coarseness, hatred, in the worst, and even in the kindest and gayest something that was tainted and heavy compared with his and Dara's. "Ours was weighted down. Yours soars."

Tormin laughed again. "Yes, your laughter is different; there is a little discord in it. But do not worry, my little daughter," he placed his hand gently on Celia's head. "It is only a shadow and will pass when you learn our ways and our thoughts and become more and more like us."

Despite Tormin's encouraging words, Celia doubted that she could ever come anywhere near to being like them. She would try her best, of course, but without losing her own personality. God certainly wouldn't want that. He had given her this individuality and would only want her to lose the bad parts that she had brought from Earth.

"Last night you said that other children had been brought from Earth. How many of us are there?"

"Ten."

"Are any my age?"

"I do not know," answered Tormin.

"We will meet them all today," said Dara who had come to call them in for the noonday meal. "We will go to the meeting place later. The seniors have summoned everyone as they wish to speak to us on some important matter. The new children will be there as well."

Celia was so excited at the prospect of meeting others from her world, perhaps someone she knew . . . perhaps even a friend from St. Lawrence High that she forgot to ask who the seniors were.

After their meal they went down to the lake where a boat was moored. It was lightweight and pointed at both ends, like a canoe. There were many boats on the lake, and as Celia took her place, she noticed that all of them were headed towards a point on this side of the lake but farther up.

Dara was in the bow of their boat with a large paddle while Tormin was in the stern. He loosed the twisted rope and with one vigorous stroke of his own even larger paddle had them clear of the shore.

As they drew nearer to the other boats, Celia eagerly searched among their occupants for the other earth children, but the ones close enough for her to see clearly held only Koinians. Ahead was a long narrow wharf of logs and stones, and as the boats converged on it greetings were called to and fro. Celia felt herself the object of all eyes and was becoming uncomfortable when she caught sight of a passenger in a boat coming up behind them. Surely that young girl in the center with the black hair and slanting eyes was Oriental. She knelt up abruptly in order to see better tipping their boat dangerously, and she dropped back onto her seat.

As they came up to the wharf Dara caught hold of it and started to moor the boat. Celia jumped out and was going to run to the other boat which had just reached the wharf, but had to stop as Dara and Tormin introduced her to several families who greeted her in the friendliest manner. Out of the corner of her eye she saw the other girl smiling and bowing her greetings happily. She seems to feel right at home, thought Celia. As they walked up the long, gradual slope Celia managed to speak to the other girl. Her name was Sumi; she came from Japan, and wasn't the Lord God good to bring them here. Celia looked back. A tall, black boy was stepping onto the wharf. We must have been taken from all over the world, she guessed.

The meeting place was a large flat area of soft turf at the

top of the slope. On either side a short distance away was a house much like Dara's and Tormin's and farther off she could see another tucked among the trees higher up the hill.

"The seniors live in them," said Dara.

All around the Koinians were settling themselves on the ground in family groups. When all had arrived Celia counted 106 adults but lost count of the many children of all ages who sat with their parents. The men and women were, like Dara and Tormin, very tall and had large quiet eyes. Their hair ranged in color from black to brown to gold with rose tints, and they all wore it the same way; the women in long braids, and the men nearly shoulder length. And all wore the same type of tunics. The colors varied, but the effect was essentially the same, a solid color with a stripe of a contrasting color from shoulder to hem. Why did they all want to look the same, thought Celia a little impatiently, and hoped that Dara would understand that earth people did not dress all alike, and would let her have a tunic that was different. Why she might start a new trend here! After all not everything on earth could have been wrong.

One of the Koinians stood up.

"He is the eldest of the seniors," Tormin told her. "The other five are beside him. Of all of us they have the most knowledge of the Lord God."

The senior did indeed look venerable in his dark blue tunic and nearly white hair though he stood erect and his voice was deep and so strong that she had no trouble hearing distinctly every word he said. As he spoke he looked over the gathering and each time his eyes fell on one of the earth children he paused and smiled. When his glance rested on her, it was so kind and warm that it made Celia feel one with the group. The other seniors were his wife and two other elderly couples who appeared to be as wise and kind as he. What surprised Celia the most was the noticeably deep joy that radiated from all of them.

"They have tidings to tell us," said Dara to her husband.

"Tidings of some great joy."

Tormin nodded. "Yes, some great knowledge has come to them."

The Koinians at once fell silent when the senior greeted them with, "Blessed be the Lord God." All answered, "Blessed is He."

The senior continued. "We all know the sorrowful story of how the spirits of Darkness tormented our forefathers, how some of them—those we now call Thabons—listened to these dark spirits and turned from the paths of God to evil ways and to hatred of us, who were once their brothers.

"But not even the Thabons have committed the evils that these spirits of Darkness taught the world from which our new children come. Evils which we now see might, in the future, have fallen upon us had not the Lord God decreed that the Thabons should decrease until none remained. Blessed be the Lord God for sparing us."

The assembly murmured, "Blessed is He."

"Yet to that earth that fell so grievously, the Lord God in His mercy and love gave a gift so great that even the spirits of Light are in wonder at it. Now to us who have taken their children, scarred with the disobedience of their First Parents, into our lives and hearts, this gift has been passed on." He paused as though unable to continue, and so great was the light and joy on his face that Celia could not look steadily at it. After a few moments he went on. "But of this gift there is one who also came from that fallen world who can tell you better than I."

He inclined his head with reverence, towards a figure she had not noticed before.

Celia stared open-mouthed then, completely forgetting where she was, jumped up crying: "Cardinal Antonio, Cardinal Antonio!" ran over to him and caught hold of his hand as though he were a port of safety in a very bewildering sea.

"Why it is Father Bruno's little friend," said the Cardinal smiling, "and these others, I know them too from my travels."

For the other earth children had also run up and were crowding around him.

"Where are we? . . . What happened? . . . Did the earth really end? . . . Where is everyone else?" the questions poured from them.

"I will speak with you later," he said after greeting them. "For the present go back to your new families."

Seven at once obeyed, but three lingered and had to be told a second time to return to their new families. They were Paul, a French-Canadian; Gian, an Italian; . . . and . . . Celia.

The Cardinal turned to the waiting Koinians. "I, too, am scarred and come from a world whose evil ways brought about its destruction, yet it is to me that God in His wisdom has given the task of bringing to you who have been faithful the Gospel that you have never heard."

There was absolute silence, not even the small children stirred, as the Cardinal told them how God, the Father, had so loved the poor planet Earth, that He sent His only Son, Jesus Christ, the Incarnate Word, to redeem it. When he spoke of the Last Supper, the Koinians understood at once the meaning of Jesus' words of Consecration, and a low murmur of wonder came from them.

"I understand now," said the Cardinal in ending, "why such a one as I was brought among you. God, the eternal Father, would not permit the memory of His Son's death and Sacrifice to pass from the universe, and since your seniors have given me permission I will now offer Mass for you."

Everything had been previously prepared. Two young Koinians brought a table which the Cardinal arranged for Mass. He called the ten earth children forward; five boys and five girls. Two of the boys served him while the other eight children knelt in front of all the people. Then he celebrated the Holy Sacrifice of the Mass, the one perfect gift that fallen, rebellious earth could give to this world that would understand and cherish it. And when the ten children bearing the shadow of that earth went forward to receive the bread and wine transformed into the Body and Blood of their Savior, the unfallen Koinians watched with love, adoration and longing.

As Celia turned from the altar she had intended to return to her original place in front of it, but found herself going, as though it were perfectly natural, towards Dara and Tormin. She knelt down between them and Dara put an arm around her, saying,

"The next time we will all three go up together."

After Mass was over the Koinians begged the Cardinal to tell them more about Jesus, the Son of God, and His teachings. He gladly did so, but soon their questions and his answers went way over Celia's head. Must be deep theology, she decided, and was very glad when all the children, those of earth and of Koinia, were sent to play while the adults remained in profound conversation.

They went to a nearby field and spent the rest of the afternoon laughing and talking like children everywhere, except that never once did Celia hear a sharp or disagreeable word, and never had she been surrounded with such friendly faces. After a while the ten newcomers were able to exchange a few words with each other. They were all about the same age and came from all over the world. The boys were from Peru, Nigeria, Phillipines, Canada and Italy; the girls from Brazil, Lebanon, Japan, Poland and the U.S.A.. None knew why he or she had been chosen nor had any of them known they were going to be saved. All came from deeply Catholic families whose lives had been centered around the Mass; some like Celia and Sumi, a descendant of the Nagasaki martyrs, had ancestors who had died for the faith.

When the Cardinal had finished speaking with the adult Koinians, he called the ten children to him. "Remember, my dear children, that we are here only by the mercy of God. Blessed be He, as they say so beautifully in this glorious land. I know that your new parents have told you that you will be given special strength and that, if you are faithful, you will one day be as close to the spirits and hearts of these holy people as it is possible for you to be."

"Yes, but what is this strength?" asked the Polish girl.

"Have you not felt it? Have not your minds become clearer and your wills stronger?"

"Yes, indeed," said Gian, the Italian. "Come to think of it, my mind has been free, free to think all the good things I have always wanted to without having my thoughts pulled where I didn't want them to go."

"That is your strength. No evil thought or desire can enter your minds and hearts without your willing it. But do not forget, you can still will these thoughts and desires. The choice for evil is still yours. Yet I know, my children," said the Cardinal as he blessed them, "that you love God and have tried to serve Him, so I do not think that direct evil will be a source of temptation for you. Be careful, and if you are troubled or in doubt, ask your parents for help, as their wisdom of God's ways is very great."

"I wouldn't risk losing this place by disobedience," said the Filipino boy. "I feel as though I had been always looking for this country and have at last come home."

"Yes, yes," cried all the children. "We will obey."

"We saw what happened to our world as a result of disobedience," said Paul, the French-Canadian, emphatically. No, none of them would disobey, Celia felt certain. They did indeed know the consequences only too well.

"Remember there are other faults besides outright disobedience," said the Cardinal slowly and firmly as though he wanted to imprint his words on their minds. "And pride is at the root of them all."

Late in the afternoon Celia climbed into the boat between Dara and Tormin, happy to be with them again. She felt she already loved them. The other earth children, she had found out, were contentedly calling their new parents father and mother.

Well, she would do the same soon, but it was nice to be different for just a little longer.

Chapter IV

The days and weeks slipped by quickly and happily. They were very full as Celia had so much to see and to learn. She soon discovered to her immense relief, that the Koinians were not, as she had feared, almost automatons, good to be sure, but automatons nevertheless guided entirely by God's directions. On the contrary, wise though they were in God's ways and lovingly obedient to Him, they evidently had direct communication with God only on extraordinary occasions, as for the coming of the earth children. The Koinians made their own plans, individually or collectively, as needed. If they forgot a tool for the work in a distant field, there was no heavenly poke to remind them. They attempted new things and sometimes failed, but without discouragement, and if another succeeded there was no resentment or envy, only pleasure at the other's success. At times they were even disappointed in their deepest desires, as had been Dara and Tormin in their wish for children. Yet never, but never, was there any questioning of God's will. Instead there was always peace, joy and contentment.

To Celia's surprise the Koinians were by no means always accurate in predicting the weather. True, the Koinia weather was changeable at this season, rapidly going from sunshine to rain and back again, but Celia for some reason had expected more accuracy. Here was something where a direct line with heaven would be useful, she thought fervently after one experience with Koinian weather.

She had made friends with many of the Koinian children, especially with Nylene, a girl her own age who lived nearby. One day she climbed with Nylene and some other children well up into the hills to collect a very delicious edible root. By this time she had learned from experience how handy her knife was. The sharp edges were used to cut twigs, vines, and the long reeds that could be quickly twisted into all sorts of serviceable things. The blunt end was used for digging herbs or roots like the ones they were collecting. Their baskets were half filled and the children were playing and talking when a loud horn sounded below them . . . once . . . twice . . . three times.

At the first blast the children stopped dead in their tracks, listening. At the third blast they grabbed their baskets and raced off at top speed down the hillside, but not by the same path they had come up.

"Quick, quick!" cried Nylene catching Celia's hand and pulling her along. "It's the maelorn. We must run to the nearest house." She shouted to the children who were vanishing down the path, "Tell them I'm coming with Celia, she can't run as fast as you." Celia tore after Nylene expecting some monster to come roaring after them, but she couldn't keep up with the others who were bounding down the slopes surefooted as mountain goats.

"What is it?" she panted looking fearfully back over her shoulder. Without answering Nylene pointed to the sky. An immense, deep red cloud, streaked heavily with black was tearing across the sky with the speed of a jet. In a few moments it had cut off the sunlight and covered the mountain with a dark shadow. The air grew chilly. The two girls were running along the top of a steep, rocky bluff when a terrific blast of wind hit them with a roar lifting Celia off of her feet and then dropping her down again. She rolled over and over and was stopped at the edge of the bluff by Nylene who flung herself forward and caught hold of her tunic.

"Lie down," she ordered. For a few minutes the wind whistled loudly over them then ceased abruptly as though cut off at its source, and Nylene jumped up and pulled Celia forward. "Lie down when the wind comes," she cried.

As Nylene went ahead down the steep, narrow path, lightning exploded from all parts of the red cloud at once and shot across the sky in a network of brilliant, red-orange streaks. Celia shrieked and crouched, frozen with fear, as peal after peal of sharp, hard thunder slammed against the mountains crashing in echoes from slope to slope. Nylene's urgent calls roused her, and she started down as fast as she could slipping and sliding recklessly. Anything to get to safety.

Without warning rain poured down like a cataract with such force that she lost her footing and fell, sliding on her back down the path. Fortunately she was almost at the bottom and the turf was soft. Celia was not hurt but could not stand up against the weight of water that held her against the ground. It stopped as suddenly as had the wind. As Nylene helped her up, they saw two men running towards them. One of the men caught Celia's arm and hurried her down the path, while the other helped Nylene. At the blasts of the wind the men made the girls lie down and knelt beside them, and then protected them from the torrents of rain by crouching over them. Once the group narrowly missed being struck by a tree that had been uprooted and fell across the path. The men pulled the girls out of its way, nevertheless Celia felt battered before they reached a house and dashed in. The other children were there in varying degrees of wetness, the slowest being the wettest, but none were as wet and muddy as Celia and Nylene. There was much friendly laughter in which Celia was able to join after she got over her fright.

"Does this maelorn come often?" she asked.

"No, no," she was assured.

"I have only seen four," said Nylene.

"They are so terrible. Why doesn't the Lord God warn you before they come?" Celia thought that surely this was a case when a little heavenly help was indicated.

"Why should He?" asked Nylene in astonishment.

Before Celia could give her reasons, one of the men opened the door, saying, "The maelorn is over," and out of the window Celia saw the red and black cloud racing across the farther mountains leaving the blue sky behind it.

Most of her new experiences, however, were pleasant. She enjoyed learning and there was much for her to learn. The Koinian's knowledge of astronomy amazed her as they did not have instruments, and yet they knew a great deal about the stars and strange forces and movements in the universe which earth's astronomers had never discovered. As Celia listened to one of the seniors who was teaching the earth children about these things, she confided to Gian, "At times I really don't know if this is a course in astronomy or religion." The senior was describing the universe as originating in an immense explosion of light that came from the Lord God and was ever traveling outwards.

"The Big Bang theory," exclaimed Paul. "These people know about it, and how many thousands of years did it take us with all our instruments to figure it out? Though actually, it is all contained in the words, 'Let there be light'."

Celia had never been very good at science and so was more interested in such things as the fall of the angels, who were changed from spirits of Light to spirits of Darkness, and their being cast out. "For," concluded the senior, "darkness cannot understand light nor can it live with light."

"That's what St. Paul said," interrupted Celia.

"St. Paul, he was one of the great teachers of the Lord Jesus, was he not?" the senior questioned the Cardinal who often attended the childrens' lessons, saying that he had as much to learn as they did. The Cardinal nodded.

"But why are you so surprised?" the senior asked Celia. "The Lord God's truths are the same in all worlds. His commands may be different, but His truths never change for they are part of Him."

"Many of us forgot that," remarked the Cardinal.

All the earth children were very impressed at the importance the Koinians gave to the spirits of Light and Darkness, and to their powers.

"Why do they?" one of the children asked the Cardinal. "We never used to hear much about either angels or devils on earth."

"That is because they understand what angels, both the good and bad ones, really are," he answered. "We had cut them down to our size until most people thought of them as amusing characters in comic strips, either with white wings and haloes, or black wings, horns and a tail. Here their tremendous powers for good or evil are well understood."

But best of all Celia liked going out with Tormin and Dara or the children and learning about the trees and shrubs and flowers, and the animals who were different from those she had known. The trees ranged from the immense ones she had seen that first night, to those six feet high with green bark and twisted, blue-gray leaves. Her favorite was a swaying willow-type of tree, whose weeping branches were covered with small flowers with petals of many shades of blue. When she stood under one it was as though she were under a huge parasol.

And the animals. Some made her laugh, such as those much like rabbits only with four long ears instead of two, and the twelve inch caterpillar that looked just like the one sitting on the mushroom in *Alice in Wonderland*. Then there were the duck sized birds whose feathers were gorgeous shades of green and yellow and who laid so many eggs that some might be taken without lessening the future number of birds.

"The mother bird lays more eggs than she can keep warm, so when you find more than six in a nest, you may take the extra ones," Tormin taught her, and he showed her how to select the freshest.

Of course, Celia (this was during her first days on Koinia) asked, "Why do the birds lay more eggs than they can hatch?"

"Do you think I know why the Lord God made them that way? Learn to thank Him instead of asking His reasons."

Gathering these eggs was the children's work and it was during one of her first searches that she discovered what had been meant by "special strength".

These birds lived in colonies and nested high in the branches of a big tree, or group of trees, if the colony were large. When they found these nests, several children would climb up, and gently lift the bird off its nest onto the branch where it stood protesting loudly. After counting the eggs, the extra ones would be removed and let down in a small basket to the children waiting below. On this particular day a boy up in the tree slipped and, in grabbing for a branch, let go of the eggs he had just collected and one of them landed on Celia's head. She had a quick temper and usually would have had to struggle to control it, but this time to her surprise, her first reaction after a gasp, was to laugh. Oh, the temper was still there. She could feel it lurking underneath, but she would have to call it up deliberately. The moment was over in a second but she made her choice and laughed while the other children sympathetically helped her to clean up.

"After all," she confided later to Dara, "who wants to call up a temper. I always felt so badly when I gave in to it."

"The more you use this strength the stronger it will grow, until all your wrong feelings and desires will be gone," Dara promised which encouraged Celia greatly.

Envy had never been one of Celia's faults and, after her first disappointment, she truly rejoiced in the superior beauty of the Koinian voices and, therefore, was delighted when the eldest senior said to her, "You have a gift for music. You must learn ours."

She clapped her hands with pleasure. "I would love to. I love music so much. How shall I start?"

"Listen to it all around you. There is music in everything: the sun, the stars, the winds, and each is different."

"We were taught that star differs from star in glory but not about their music."

"Each has its own song of praise to the Lord God."

"But I can't hear them," wailed Celia. To love music so much, to know that it was all around, and not to be able to hear it, she could have wept in frustration.

"Then listen to the silence; that too is beautiful," answered the senior.

"But I want to hear the music so much," she said desperately.

"The Teacher-of-the-Lord-Jesus—that is what the Koinians called the Cardinal—has told me of the endless noise of your earth. Listen with your heart. Let go of your world; let its noise fade, then you will hear our music. And who can teach you better than your father and mother. They hear it so well. Few among us hear it better."

This confirmed Celia's suspicions that Dara and Tormin were considered special even among these extraordinarily wonderful people—and they had been chosen for her; this was a pleasant thought. It was only much later that it occurred to her that she might have been given to them because she needed special help. She managed to shove the thought aside, reassuring herself, that she would never have been brought to Koinia if she were a real problem. No, she was just a little different.

Dara and Tormin were her main teachers, and she was happiest when with them. Tormin showed her how to make pottery, but despite her best efforts, she showed no aptitude for that art, and could only help him in small ways, such as mixing the clay. To Dara's delight, however, she showed a real ability for weaving.

"Sing," Dara would say. "Sing, and then your work will

flow with the music. Choose a song that fits the pattern and then the melody will be woven into it." Celia could see the results in Dara's designs; each one had its own rhythm.

Soon Dara said she could weave a length of tunic material for herself. Celia had been waiting for this opportunity. The sameness of all the tunics still irked her, and she felt that the only way to convince Dara how pretty another pattern could be, would be to show her one.

After the warp had been set up, Celia wove a few inches in the main color, and then when Dara was busy with other work, laid skeins of different colors in an attractive design on top of the warp. She certainly would not do anything disobedient, she told herself, but it could not be disobedience to merely show a new color scheme without actually weaving it in. One often did that in weaving. Dara did it herself. When the skeins were arranged to her liking, she asked Dara to look at it.

"Don't you think a tunic would be handsomer in this new design rather than always using the other one? In my world our clothing was all sorts of shapes and colors."

"That was on your earth which is gone," said Dara. "Here," and for the first time Celia heard a sternness in her voice, "you must do as we do." And with a quick movement she swept the skeins from the loom.

"But why?" protested Celia.

Dara started to speak, then stopped. "That I may not tell you. It is something the Lord God wishes you to learn by yourself."

So Celia obediently, if disappointedly, wove a deep green tunic with pale green stripes and made an effort, though not a wholehearted one, to be pleased with the result. What reason could there possibly be for keeping to this sameness except an unwillingness to change? They've done the same thing for so long, they're probably in a bit of a rut, she thought.

It was the same thing with the braids that all the women and girls wore. Celia's hair, which had been short when she came, was growing rapidly. When Dara mentioned one day that it was almost long enough to braid, Celia again silently rebelled. Not that she considered it rebellion, merely a bit of exasperation at that eternal sameness. She would braid it if told to, but she convinced herself that if she fixed her hair attractively before she was actually ordered to braid it, she might be allowed to wear it the way she wanted to. That night before going to bed, she carefully trimmed her hair, keeping it long, but stylishly shaped and curled. In the morning she combed it out, and arranged it as becomingly as she could without a mirror, and then went into the kitchen, not without some trepidation.

"Look, Dara mother and Tormin father, I thought you might like to see one of the ways we did our hair. This is only one style. There were dozens and dozens of others." There was silence as they looked at her.

"Was that your only reason?" Tormin asked her very quietly.

"No," Celia answered honestly. "I did it because I hoped that when you saw how becoming it was, you would let me do my hair this way instead of braiding it like everyone else."

"Why," continued Tormin, again very quietly, "did you not want to be like everyone else?"

Celia said nothing and lowered her eyes. The silence in the kitchen was intense. She wished he would scold her, anything except this waiting silence. At last she looked up unhappily. "I did it to feel special and so that everyone would see that I was different."

"Everyone is different. Everyone is special; you need to learn that. Do not do such a thing again, my daughter," and there was that in his voice which made her, as soon as the meal was over, hurry to the nearest water jar, comb in hand. She returned a few minutes later with her hair straight and dripping.

"Dara mother," she said contritely. "Please show me how to braid my hair the way you do."

It was not, she had to admit to herself, that the Koinians

refused to learn anything new that came from the earth. When she had cautiously described to Dara the difference between her loom and Aunt Mattie's, Dara had been very interested and with Tormin's help had made some changes on her loom. Paul, she knew, had shown them how to make a very useful tool, and no parent had objected in the slightest when the Brazilian girl had taught their delighted children the intricacies of jump rope.

Celia sighed occasionally, but did not forget that she was on probation, so to speak, and firmly resolved not to try to be different except where it was permitted. Therefore, she still did not call Dara and Tormin mother and father, even though she loved them dearly and obeyed them promptly and happily. Without realizing it, this refusal had become a symbol of what she felt was her vanishing identity, a forlorn flag which she had nailed to the mast of her independence. After all, she reminded her conscience, they themselves had suggested "Dara mother" and "Tormin father", and how much more musical those terms were than plain "mother" and "father"—someday perhaps, she would change. And so, though she sighed sometimes, she conformed at least outwardly. There again the thought that this merely surface conformity might be a form of rebellion never entered her head.

Chapter V

As time passed Celia learned and found joy in learning. This happiness was one of the big differences between the people of the earth and those of this world. Everything here was done with joy, even the most difficult and wearying tasks. There was none of "I can't stand this job, but I've got to do it," attitude. Whether the Koinians worshipped or worked or played, they did it with joy because it was the right thing to do in their God-oriented lives, and therefore it was good and something to be enjoyed. Nothing Celia had ever heard of even in the lives of the saints compared with this.

Once when she was with a group working in the communal fields, a youngster ran up saying that two of the betans, the pony sized wool bearing animals whose fleece was used for weaving, had fallen into a bog. Several of the men, Tormin among them, hurried to the animals' rescue, and a long, hot muddy process it was; the poor animals struggled so. Yet not a grumble or cross word came from the men even though, at the end, they were dirty, scratched, and weary. They flung themselves down in the shade for a brief rest; then with a kind word and pat to the animals who were now grazing contentedly, they went back to their work in the fields.

"Tormin father," Celia exclaimed. "Don't you ever get annoyed when things go wrong?"

"Annoyed?" Tormin thought a moment as though the word was not familiar to him. By now Celia knew the Koinians well enough, and Tormin in particular, not to suspect even for a moment that he was pretending not to understand.

"You mean, my little daughter, the way you felt yesterday when you wanted to go off with the other children and your mother needed your help?"

Celia nodded grudgingly. She had thought that she had been able to conceal her feelings. "Well, yes."

Another man, Gian's father, said matter-of-factly as though he were mentioning the learning of simple sums, "Yes, our new children must learn that doing the right thing at the right moment, whether it is work or prayer or play, is what brings joy. Then all the shadows will be gone from their lives and all the—what was that word—annoyance, also. But they will learn. Gian is learning already." He smiled in a fatherly manner at Celia. "And then what knowledge they have brought us."

This remark started the men talking about the building they were constructing in order that the Great Gift, as they called the Blessed Sacrament, might have a dwelling as fitting as they could make it. Everyone considered it a privilege to share in the work. The older children eagerly did what they could and, when some of the smaller children were found crying because they were not big enough to help, they were given the task of keeping full the jars of drinking water for the workers. Since they were only able to carry small containers and slopped a great deal of the water as they brought it from the nearby spring, this task kept them happily busy.

Except for Gian, the Italian boy, who lived nearby, Celia did not often have a chance to speak with the other earth children, as some of them lived across the lake, and others much farther up the shore. But when they did meet, she realized with considerable mortification that those from the poorer and culturally less important countries were adjusting more quickly than herself, whose nation had been the wealthiest and most powerful her lost world had ever known. One by one she saw a new look come into their eyes, a reflection, slight to be sure, but unmistakable of that deep peace and joy-without-shadow of the Koinians. At length only four of them did not yet have it. The Japanese girl, Sumi, was one. She admitted that she found some things difficult but said very earnestly, that she was going to try harder. She must have, for soon she too, had this Koinian look as Celia called it.

"What's wrong with us?" Gian said to Celia and Paul.

"Well," said Paul straightforwardly, "I know what's wrong with me. It's not being allowed to even hope of going beyond those mountains and far down the river. Here I am a descendant of those intrepid *voyageurs* who explored the wilds of Canada, surrounded by unknown lands such as I never dreamed existed, and am told that I can't leave this valley. I feel like a hunting dog chained to a kennel who hears the hunt go by."

"Why can't you leave this valley?" asked Gian in surprise.

"Because some of those Thabons who rebelled against the Lord God might still be around."

"Why does that matter?" questioned Celia. "Part of the Thabons punishment was to decrease until none remained. If there are any left, everyone says they must be very few."

"That's not it," explained Paul. "The Koinians know that the Thabons in their hatred and envy would do them evil if possible, while they still look on the Thabons as brothers and will do nothing that might incite them to attack. 'We would defend ourselves,' my father says, 'but will not give them the opportunity to do more evil.' And so I'll have to wait until it is certain that no Thabons are left . . . and that probably won't be until I'm old and tottering. All I can do is wonder what's beyond those mountains and way down the river and keep on feeling like that chained dog." But he laughed as he said this, and added, "Like Sumi, I'm just going to have to try harder." He waved his hand and went off singing.

"That leaves just the two of us," Gian said gloomily to Celia. "What's troubling you?"

"There's so much sameness in some things. I don't want the me that was to be totally submerged and changed into something completely new." She brought out her pet argument. "After all God, I mean the Lord God, did give me my own identity, and He must want me to keep at least the good parts."

"I don't have any trouble with that," Gian said with a grin. "I'm me, and I'll always be me, a better me I hope someday, but still me. What does get under my skin is that I have no hope of ever doing anything as well as they can. Sing, swim, climb . . . whatever it is, they can do it better. They have only to touch something and it's better or more beautiful. Look at what they've managed to do with the Mass in a few weeks. Two thousand years on earth never produced results like that."

Celia agreed understandingly. "I know what you mean."

The Sacrifice of the Mass had at once become the center of the Koinian's worship. They had insisted on baptism before receiving Communion though the Cardinal said they did not need it. "The Lord Jesus was baptised," they had answered and that ended the matter.

The prayers of the Mass were revised by a group of the best poets, musicians and deepest thinkers who had composed a new Mass, keeping the words of Consecration, but little else. The first time the new Liturgy was celebrated Celia was overwhelmed by its beauty. The words and music soared up to heaven then dropped back in a murmur. Back and forth it went until the Koinians had a listening look on their faces as though they heard something she could not.

Adoration, Reparation, Petition and Thanksgiving, the four traditional parts of the Mass had been kept. Adoration and Thanksgiving were as natural as breathing to the Koinians; Petition had had a place in their worship though in a very selfless form, but Reparation for sin had been a new concept to them, though one they had grasped so eagerly that Cardinal Antonio was astonished.

"You don't need to make reparation," he told them.

"That is true," one of them had replied, "but now that we know what terrible evils there were in your world, we realize that there may be other worlds where the Lord God has been deeply offended and where the inhabitants need our prayers."

Thus all four parts of the Mass were included, yet it seemed to Celia that in the end all were merged into the only one that would last for eternity—Adoration.

Nor was there any fear of losing the Mass because two of the young men had promptly attached themselves to the Cardinal. "My seminary," he called them laughingly, "though I am learning as much from them as they from me."

Not every activity was learning or work no matter how enjoyable. There were times for play, plenty of them. The Koinians loved anything to do with water. They swam like fish, played water games, ran rapids in their boats and spent much of their free time in or on the water. Gian and Celia often met at a cove where many of the children gathered to swim. It had a nice beach, while along the shore were straight steep banks and deep water.

"Strange, isn't it," observed Gian when they were swimming one afternoon, "that while these Koinians are such magnificent swimmers, they know only the simplest sort of dive, and I can't say they do even that very well. I've got an idea."

"What is it?"

"Wait and see," was all Gian would say with a big chuckle.

The next time she came to the cove Gian was putting the finishing touches on a simple but sturdy diving board on a bank high above the deep water. He went out to the end and bounced up and down.

"Perfect," he shouted happily. Then he paced back, turned, took three running steps and did a swan dive. He was an excellent fancy diver. To the shouts and applause of the children, he did a front and back jack knife, twists, gainers; he knew all sorts of dives. The other children begged for lessons and soon were hitting the water in the wild positions usual with beginners. Their shouts and laughter drew adults who were just as enthusiastic in trying, and also just as awkward as the children. Gian explained and demonstrated until he was so tired that he could only sit on the bank and pant, but he was beaming. Celia was happy for him. At last there was something in which he excelled and would be content. He didn't quite have the Koinian look, but he was so happy that she was certain he would the next time they met. That leaves only me, she thought miserably as she walked home.

She did not see Gian for a while. Dara had been one of the expert weavers chosen to make hangings for the Great Gift building and Celia was busy helping her prepare and dye the necessary wool. When they did meet again at the cove, to Celia's surprise Gian did not look a bit contented. He was sitting on the bank gazing glumly at the swimmers.

"See," he said to her, pointing to the diving board. "What did I tell you? Some of them are already diving as well as I can. Look at that!" He jerked his head toward a young man who was doing a gainer. Up he went, tucked himself into a perfect somersault then came out of it in a graceful dive. A girl followed with a beautiful jack knife.

Celia had difficulty understanding his attitude. "But, Gian, weren't there many divers on earth who were better than you?" Surely Gian didn't think that he was that good.

"Of course," he said impatiently. "Quantities of them. That's not the problem. I could always hope that with lots of practice I might one day be as good as they were, but not here. They will always be better in everything. Could you imagine anyone on earth being able to do a gainer as well as that only two weeks after beginning to learn to dive? In another two weeks some of them will be better than the Olympic champions."

"They're certainly learning fast," she had to admit. She felt sorry for Gian, he was usually so cheerful and fun loving but could not share his problem.

"Paul's all right now. Just you and I aren't. We're misfits, that's what we are, misfits!" Gian burst forth.

Misfits.

Celia's heart sank and a chill went through her. If they were indeed misfits they would not be allowed to stay. All this beauty, all this happiness would be taken away from her, Dara and Tormin as well. At this thought she jumped up and ran back home as fast as she could, for Dara and Tormin were her world and the love with which they surrounded her was her security. Never had she imagined that two persons with such distinct personalities could love each other so selflessly with a love that really made them one. So close had they grown that often they had no need of words to know what the other was thinking or needing. One evening when the two of them were sitting together looking out over the lake, Dara with her head on Tormin's shoulder, Celia had told them, "Our Lady and St. Joseph must have loved each other the way you do."

"Ah, no," exclaimed Dara. "There was only one love like theirs," for the Koinians had at once given the Holy Family a special place in their hearts. But Celia could see that Dara and Tormin were pleased at her remark.

Yet, though she knew that they truly loved her as a daughter, she had managed to convince herself that a third person, especially someone from another world, would be an intruder. Besides, here her spirit of independence had raised its head again, she did not want to be submerged in that love, though deep in her heart she knew, or would have known if she had let herself, that a love as selfless as Tormin's and Dara's would not engulf, but uphold her.

This day as she ran home in fear of losing them, all this went through her mind. She would make amends; she would start calling them mother and father at once. She dashed into the house. Neither of them was there nor anywhere nearby. Perhaps Dara was with Nylene's mother who was an expert spinner, so she ran back along the path and up the slope to-wards Nylene's house. On the way she met Nylene and her younger brother.

"Why are you running so fast, Celia?" asked Nylene. "Do come with us. We're going to pick roseberries."

Celia stopped, panting. Roseberries were delicious; fat as big cherries and deep rose colored when fully ripe, and with a sweet flavor unlike any fruit on earth. What a good idea! She would fill two baskets and so have a gift each for Dara and Tormin when she first called them mother and father.

"I'll run and get a basket, Nylene. Where are you going to pick them?"

"Up near the big rocks; the berries there should be ripe by now."

"I know a much better place beyond the last house on this side of the lake. Tormin father and I passed it yesterday. The bushes were full of huge berries, most of them ripe."

"It's too late to go that far," said Nylene, "and there are plenty up this way, I'm sure."

Celia was about to insist when Nylene's young brother said, "Why do you say 'Tormin father'? It's so ugly."

Celia was taken back. "It's not ugly. On the contrary, it's very musical to say 'Tormin father, Dara mother'."

"No, it isn't," insisted the youngster. "There's no music in it. It's like this." Waving one hand rhythmically and slashing across its movement with the other, he expressively conveyed a sense of discord.

Celia was about to reply when she saw from Nylene's expression that Nylene thought the same, though she tried to cover it up by hastily saying, "We'll go ahead. Get your basket and join us."

Really shaken, Celia walked slowly down to her house. Discord. If it was wrong why had she been told to use Dara mother and Tormin father on that very first day? Why? . . . it came to her suddenly that it was her attitude that made the dis-

cord, not the words. This realization upset her even more. All
the Koinians must have noticed it; a disharmony was the sort of
thing they sensed at once. She could understand why Dara and
Tormin might feel they could not tell her, but why hadn't
someone else? One of the seniors, anyone. She would have
stopped right away. Celia found two baskets and started back up
the path. "Misfit" echoed and re-echoed through her whole being. Nylene was her friend, she should have warned her. Why
hadn't she? . . . why hadn't she?

Annoyed with Nylene and feeling a little resentful, Celia
came to a fork in the path; to the left led up to the rocks where
Nylene was waiting for her; to the right to the spot where she
had seen the big roseberries yesterday. They would probably be
much riper than those at the rocks, and, after all, she was under
no obligation to obey Nylene. In this she could do as she
pleased. Celia hesitated for a moment, then chose the right hand
path. The bushes she had noticed were a good distance away,
but she hurried, certain that she could fill both baskets and get
back home before Dara and Tormin—and before Nylene too.
Wait until she sees my baskets, Celia thought.

The small hollow, warm in the afternoon sun, was full of
the grey leaved bushes, whose arching branches were weighted
with berries that looked like rose jewels. She picked as rapidly
as she could with an eye on the downward path of the sun. As
soon as one basket was filled she set it down and started on the
second working her way across the hollow. When she neared
the other side she was vaguely aware of voices but at first paid
no attention to them. Slowly they penetrated her consciousness
until she stopped picking to listen. Something was wrong with
those voices. She listened intently. Harshness, that's what it was;
but there wasn't a harsh voice among the Koinians. In fact, she
had almost forgotten what a harsh voice sounded like.

She crept up the farther slope and peered through the
bushes. Below her, near the edge of the lake, a man and woman
were talking. The first thing she noticed about them was that

their clothes were many colors and very bright. For a moment Celia thought that they were more people from her own earth and was about to cry out in welcome, when she saw their faces. No earth humans had those large eyes, only Koinians . . . and Thabons. That must be who they were; so some were still left after all. They were too far away for her to hear clearly what they were saying, only a few words here and there . . . "attack . . . houses." All she could think of was of Dara sitting at her loom quietly singing and Thabons breaking in, knives in hand . . . She must warn the Koinians. Frantic with fear she began to creep quietly backwards down the slope, terrified of making a noise that would alert the man and woman.

Chapter VI

An iron hand seized her shoulder. She was pulled to her feet then thrown to the ground. Bruised and frightened she screamed only to be again dragged to her feet and struck heavily across the face.

"Stop that," snarled a brutal voice. Dazed, she looked up and saw a cruel hard face twisted with coarse laughter. "Get up." With her head still ringing from the blow Celia pulled herself to her knees. The Thabon slapped her across the face again but not so hard this time, and caught hold of her and slung her across his shoulders like a sack. He carried her to where the other two were sitting and dropped her on the bank.

"Caught her spying on us," he said.

"Probably thought she could warn the others," grunted the other man. "Let's see what more we can get before she's missed."

"Too late," said her captor. "There were two baskets. Her friend must have run back while this one kept watch on us." He aimed a kick at Celia which, fortunately, only grazed her.

The three Thabons argued angrily. Her captor appeared to be the leader, at least he talked the loudest and most aggressively. The woman agreed with him in sharp, shrill tones until the other man reluctantly gave in. He took his disappointment out on Celia.

"Get up," he yelled at her with a threatening gesture. "Carry our things down to the boat."

There was nothing to do except obey which she did as slowly as possible, heartsick with worry over the words "what more can we get?" Dara often visited the last house just a short way back up the hill. Had they been there? The Thabons' boat was drawn up out of the water and beside it were bundles thrown this way and that. Someone with eyes half closed was lying among them.

"Gian," she exclaimed in dismay. He opened his eyes slowly and appeared to have difficulty in focusing them. The Thabons were doing something to the hull and still talking angrily among themselves, so Celia knelt beside him and whispered, "Gian, it's Celia. What happened? How did you get caught?"

A dreadful long black bruise was forming across the left side of his face, and from what she could see of the welts that were reddening, he must have had a really rough beating. He licked dry lips and tried to speak. Celia saw a cup among the scattered articles. Keeping an eye on the Thabons she dipped cool water from the lake and poured it over his face. He sat up with an effort. She refilled the cup and he drank eagerly.

"What happened, Gian?" she repeated.

He looked at her miserably. "I left the swimming place right after you did. I was terribly upset. I knew I was in the wrong and went for a long walk to think things over. When I saw these people I guessed at once they were Thabons and saw from what they were carrying that they had been looting. They didn't see me and I was going to run back and warn the Koinians when I saw them dump their things and go back for more. I knew the right thing to do was to let the Koinians take care of the matter, but I thought, here at last was something I could do that the Koinians couldn't. I, Gian, could prevent the Thabons from getting away by making a hole in their boat . . . I would be a hero. So I did the wrong thing and, of course, was caught." Here his voice became so sad that it tore Celia's heart. "Now

I've lost everything! All this happiness, all this love."

There was no time to say anything more. The Thabons shoved the boat back into the water and told the children to get in. Gian struggled to get up but fell back, and he was picked up and dropped in. When Celia tried to stall, the leader grabbed her arm, flipped her over the side of the boat, and sent her sprawling onto the bottom. The bundles and baskets were dumped in around them, and Celia heard Gian give a stifled moan when something hit him.

The Thabons climbed in, the woman in front, the leader in the center and the other man in the stern. They paddled rapidly. Despairingly Celia watched the shore with the friendly houses dotted here and there slide farther away as they headed to where the lake flowed away into a broad river. She tried to comfort herself with the thought that surely Dara must be safe, for the Thabons spoke among themselves only of the looting, and not of meeting any Koinians, but her heart ached for Dara and Tormin and their love. That love was far greater than any she had known on earth, loving though Aunt Mattie had been. Dara mother and Tormin father, she wept because she had never called them mother and father though she had well known they longed for her to do so and, as she now realized, too late, she wanted to more than anything else. Even her decision that afternoon to change had been through fear, a fear of her own loss rather than a desire to please them and show her love for them. In her smug wish to be different—why had she thought that important—she had only succeeded in being selfish and, like Gian, had thrown everything away, for she had no illusions that the Thabons would ever let them go. She had been tried and found wanting; she had failed God, failed Dara and Tormin, and failed herself.

The movement of the leader's arm in front of her as he paddled focused her attention on their many colored clothes. How coarse, gaudy—in a flash everything was clear.

Of course she was meant to keep her own identity, not

only to keep it but to develop it to its full potentiality. That was the true meaning of being different, not exterior trivialities which only too often were used as attention getters or to cover up inadequacies. The Koinians, on the contrary, were never sidetracked; they always saw straight to the heart of things. At last she understood. As the plain walls showed off the beauty of the hangings, so the plain tunics and hair styles set off not only the nobility of the Koinians and the gracefulness of their movements, but also, in a way, the distinct individuality and personality of each one. How often on earth had she looked at the fashionable clothes rather than at the person; or at the expensive outfit, the current hairstyle, the showy walk, even though she knew perfectly well that the wearer's life was anything but admirable. How utterly stupid and blind and selfish she had been.

The leader turned to speak to the man in the stern and gave one of his loud laughs when he saw her crying.

"Keep it back for later. You'll have more to cry about then."

A shiver of fear went through her. "What are you going to do with us?"

"Slaves. We're the last of the Thabons and we're going to a place far away where the two of you can spend your lives serving us. If any of your relatives," he gave another crude laugh, "try to rescue you, they'll see you killed in a way neither of you will like."

The Thabon behind her also laughed and kicked her. She gave a cry that was as much of anguish of heart as of pain, which brought more laughter, but the leader told the other not to hurt her too much. "She's got a lot of walking to do. We can't carry both of them."

Helplessly she watched the shores of the river go by and tried to figure out how long it would be before Dara and Tormin and Gian's parents grew worried and started to search for them. It might be hours she thought miserably. If the couple

who lived in the looted house were at work in one of the farther fields they might not even discover what had happened until tomorrow. She wondered how badly Gian was hurt and
wished she could do something for him, but he was in the front
part of the boat. He seemed to be better as he was sitting up.
Once he turned around, caught her glance, and gave her a quick
wink.

The boat was shipping water and towards sunset so much
had come in that the Thabons ran it ashore and told Gian and
Celia to get out while they mended it.

"I made those holes," Gian managed to whisper with a faint
grin. She knew he was trying to cheer her up.

"Good for you," she whispered back. "Maybe we'll sink in
the middle of the river, and then we might be able to make a
break for freedom," though she knew there was no hope of
that, the Thabons would drown them before letting them get
away.

The Thabons quickly mended the leak, shoved the children back into the boat and went on. The sun set and reviving
cool air blew across her hot face. Surely by now she and Gian
had been missed and the hunt was on. When her two baskets
were found would the Koinians notice the marks where the
boat had been drawn up and guess what had happened? At least
when they found the looted house they would know but when
would that be? How long would it take a rescue party to get
started, and would they know which way to go? She braced her
hopes by imagining that the Koinians were already on the way,
and from the Thabons' conversation knew that they were wondering the same thing.

Dip, dip, dip went the paddles. Surely they would soon
have to stop and rest, but they did not. The Thabons pulled out
food from a bundle and ate while paddling but did not give the
children any. Night fell and finally Celia's eyes closed from
sheer weariness. She was jolted awake when the boat was again
run ashore, but the Thabons stopped only long enough to rear-

range the bundles so that they could take turns sleeping. She and Gian were made to sit back to back with their knees bent so as to give more room to the Thabon whose turn it was to rest. This position was terribly uncomfortable, and when they were told to resume their former places, they were so stiff that they had difficulty straightening out their legs.

Dawn came with its rose colors and cloudless sky presaging another hot day. It was not long before her head ached and spots danced in front of her eyes whether she had them open or shut. She and Gian were still given nothing to eat, and as there had been no halt since the evening before, there had been no chance to get a drink either, and Celia was very thirsty.

In a small pouch at her belt she always kept the rosary Aunt Mattie had given her long ago, and she fingered it whenever she thought no one was looking. Their knives had already been taken from them, and she reasoned the Thabons would probably take anything she had just out of spite. The feel of the beads comforted her a little. "Blessed Mother, please help us," she prayed over and over.

Loud voices made her open her eyes. The Thabons were arguing and after a while they stopped paddling, but continued arguing. The boat was close to the left shore which was unusually rocky, until then the banks had been mostly turf or clay.

"Here's the place, just as I remember it," announced the leader.

"Are you sure?" asked the woman sharply. "You were a child when you were here."

With a sinking feeling in the pit of her stomach Celia realized that they were planning to leave the river. How would the Koinians ever find them if they did?

"I know I'm right," said the leader, angrily driving one fist into the palm of his other hand. "I've got a memory for places. And if there's a rescue party coming, they'll never think we went this way. Sure, they probably know about this crossing, but they'll guess that we'll keep to the river so as to get away as fast as we can. If they stop to look, these stones will cover our tracks."

In the end he convinced the other two and the boat was run into the shallows and Celia and Gian ordered to get out. Gian had difficulty and stumbled.

"You help him," said the woman giving Celia such a push that she fell to her knees and scraped them badly which caused the usual laughter. How she hated the sound of it. At least she and Gian were able to have a good drink while the Thabons were pulling the boat out of the river. They told the children to walk in front and the three Thabons followed carrying the boat filled with bundles. Celia, helping Gian, started up the rocky bed of a long dried out stream.

"Our feet will leave no marks, and the Koinians don't have dogs to track us; they'll keep on going down the river," Celia said despairingly to Gian, and hope nearly left her. Ahead the pebbled gulch ended and the forest began. She slipped her hand into her pouch and clutched the rosary. "Blessed Mother," she begged, "let them come before it's too late." She twisted her head for one last look at the river. Empty. Her movement caught the leader's attention.

"They're not going to find you. We'll see to that. What's in that bag at your belt?"

Reluctantly Celia took out her rosary. The Thabon yanked it from her hand. "What's this?" he snarled. His expression was hideous. Celia was so frightened that she could not answer. He examined the rosary. When he came to the crucifix his face became contorted with hatred, and he flung it away as though it had burnt him. "Get on," he howled.

"He's never seen a rosary or crucifix and yet he hates both of them," she said to Gian. Strangely this made her feel a little better.

"Remember the senior said a universal truth that darkness cannot stand the Light," Gian said. He managed a smile. "These Thabons are darkness all right!"

It was a long portage. Celia had been a good tracker in the Girl Scouts and automatically watched for landmarks as they were marched along . . . two fallen trees, a flat topped boulder, a small bank with water trickling down it. . . .

Gian was beginning to lurch from side to side, soon she could no longer hold him up. The Thabons dumped him into the boat and a sack was taken out and given to Celia to carry. This made the going harder for her and it was not long before she too began to stumble from weariness and hunger. By now the Thabons were grumbling at their leader.

"We're lost," they complained. "You don't know where you're going. We ought to go back to the other river while there's still time."

"I know I'm right," he yelled back at them. "Keep on. It's the prisoners that are slowing us down."

"Let's get rid of them," said the second man stopping abruptly. Celia was so exhausted she flopped down where she stood while they argued. It turned into a yelling contest.

"No, I want the slaves to work for me," shrilled the woman.

"Slaves and revenge," said the leader viciously. Celia was prodded to her feet and they went on.

Not long afterwards the forest ended and they stood on the banks of a river larger than the one they had left. The leader was triumphantly scornful of the other Thabons and the second man reluctantly admitted that crossing over to this river had been a good idea. The boat was dropped into the water and they all clambered in. Gian seemed better for the rest, but Celia was frightened by his white face.

This time she was in the front of the boat and the leader who was behind her amused himself by jabbing her with his foot. Her back was soon covered with bruises, and she had to bite her lips to keep from crying out when he hit a sore spot.

All at once they began to argue again, but less fiercely this time. Ahead the river forked sharply, with one branch going off to the right, and the other to the left. The argument was over which branch to follow.

"To the left," shouted the leader. "I know. I'm the only one who's been here. I was right about the crossing, wasn't I?"

The second man contradicted him automatically rather than with any conviction and was quickly overridden, and on they went. The hot sun was directly in front of them and the glare from the water was so bright that Celia kept her head down and so did the Thabons, particularly the woman who was in the bow. Not that it mattered as the river swept them along smoothly.

She was jerked upright by a shattering scream of fear. In an instant the Thabons had swung around and were paddling violently back upstream against the strong current. Hope surged through Celia; they had seen Koinians. The Thabons were nearly hysterical and strained at their paddles.

One of them howled, "Out with them," and the next instant Celia was seized and thrown into the river just missing a jagged rock, but this rock was her salvation. As she struggled to the surface choking and gasping, the current pushed her against it and instinctively she clutched its rough sides. Something bumped against her. It was Gian feebly trying to swim. Keeping one arm around the rock, she managed to catch hold of him and, again helped by the current, pulled him against the rock.

"Hang on!" she shouted, and he dazedly managed to do so. Her kicking feet struck a ledge. She stood up, and got an arm around Gian until his floundering feet also found a foothold.

Only seconds had passed since she had been thrown in, but despite their desperate efforts the Thabons were being swept downstream by the strong current. Celia felt Gian slipping and once more managed to pull him to the ledge. As she did she heard the Thabons' yells turn into one long hideous shriek, and when she looked up there was no sign of them. They've capsized, she thought frantically, suppose they reach this rock, . . . they'll drag us off. Then she heard the noise, a dull vast roar—she had heard that sound before—where? For a moment her stunned mind refused to function, then the answer came . . . Niagara Falls. A river of water falling from immense height onto more water and rocks below—and three shrieking Thabons in a boat hurtling down, down, down.

Horrified, she pressed her face against the rock and stood shuddering until Gian's voice brought her back.

"How do we get to shore?" The cold water had revived him, and he was able to stand without her help. She didn't think that he guessed about the falls and didn't tell him; one terrified person was enough.

Their rock was one of several tumbled together in the river. Most of them were jagged like the one they were clinging to, but near the bank was a boulder with a large, flat top well above the water.

"Let's get to that rock," she gasped, the pull of the current was tiring her. "There we can at least get out of the river."

Together they managed to reach it by hauling themselves from rock to rock. Gian tried gamely, but she had to help him clamber up onto the flat rock, then pulled herself up and collapsed beside him while the river swirled by, then plunged and roared out of sight.

A long while afterwards, she lifted her head and looked around. They were close to the bank which at this point jutted out in a mass of huge boulders. From their perch she could see under the water two long flat rocks that stretched to the bank like a submerged causeway. She shook Gian gently.

"I'm going to try the current. You stay here." Before he could protest, she slid over the edge into the water, holding firmly onto the rock. She almost laughed with relief. The water only came up to her knees and had no more strength than a quiet eddy. She waded to the shore testing every step, then went back. Gian was sitting up and greeted her with a gay though weak wave.

"Don't worry about me. Take care of yourself, I'll make it."

But he was leaning heavily on her by the time they reached the bank, yet after scrambling up he would not stop. "Come on. If we hide among those trees, perhaps they won't find us."

Then Celia told him what had happened to the Thabons. From this height they could see the lip of the falls and beyond it a deep gorge.

Gian sank to the ground and leaned back against a tree with a sigh of relief, "They said they were the last of the Thabons. Now the Koinians are safe forever. Well, whatever happens to us, Blessed be the Lord God."

"Blessed is He," finished Celia.

The sun was well past noon when they felt rested enough to go on. Gian was still dreadfully white and one side of his face was black and swollen and they were both weak from hunger.

"Are you badly hurt, Gian?"

"When they caught me putting holes in their boat one of them hit me on the side of the head with a paddle, and I get dizzy when I stand up. If we could find something to eat, I'd feel better."

"Don't get up," said Celia. "I'll hunt for food."

Gian closed his eyes while she searched, but she found nothing she dared eat. Disappointed she returned. Gian was standing up and insisted that he felt better and that they ought to start back.

"We've got to get to the other river."

They kept close to the bank where there was little undergrowth and the moss-covered ground felt soft under their feet. By and by they came to a grove of luscious, fully ripe roseberries which greatly refreshed them. Gian was cheerful but soon had to stop and rest; in a few minutes he went on, but then had to stop again. Then he was having to rest more and more frequently and for longer and longer periods. Finally he said quietly, "Celia, I can't go any farther. You leave me here and go on."

"I won't leave you, I won't," she said determinedly.

"You've got to. Can't you see that our only chance is to reach the other river before the Koinians get to the spot where we crossed over to this one. I know there's not much hope, but it may have been hours and hours before they found out what happened and started after us."

"But I can't leave you alone," Celia sobbed.

"I won't be alone," he said very gently. "And whatever happens to me now doesn't matter because I know I belong here."

On his face Celia saw the Koinian look, that peace that had come to the other earth children, and though she did not know it, Gian saw the same light on hers.

"We're no longer misfits," he said.

She bent down and kissed him on the forehead and each cheek. "I'll go."

The shadows were lengthening and she went as fast as she could, half walking, half trotting, looking eagerly for the grotesquely twisted tree she had noticed near the start of the crossing; but she couldn't keep up the pace and soon had to slow down to a walk, and then to stop a few minutes before continuing.

Hungry and weary, she watched the sun sink with growing fear. It had set, but the sky was still light when she at last came to the twisted tree. She paused to catch her breath, then plunged into the woods, part of which were already in deep shadows. If night came before she got through to the other river she wouldn't be able to see her landmarks, so she hurried on desperately. There was that tall, white tree, good . . . where was the mound of rocks? . . . oh, there it was. She was too far to the left and swerved to the right. The trees closed overhead cutting off almost all of the last light in the sky. She managed to see another marker, a large rotten stump, before the dark turned the trees into black masses she could barely see. Frightened and feeling as though her chest was bursting, she plunged on, gasping, until she ran into something hard and solid with water trickling over it. That must be the little bluff, but it should have been on her right. . . . She wasn't much more than halfway to the other river. Panting and stumbling with her hands in front of her she went on, only to trip and fall, pick herself up and trip again. All around was blackness or was that because she was getting lightheaded? Gian would die unless she went faster. Blindly she started to run, crashed headlong into a tree and fell stunned. She lay with her face deep in the moss and was trying to pull herself together when she felt herself being lifted up and in the flickering lights of the torches around her saw Tormin's face.

"Father, father," she sobbed, clinging to him while he held her close. "Is mother safe?"

"She is right here, my little daughter. She would not let me go without her," and another pair of loving arms went around Celia.

After the rescue party had hurried on to find Gian, Celia tried to say how sorry she was, but they kissed her and said, "Let the past be forgotten in the past. Now we have a real daughter."

While Tormin started a fire and Dara tended her cuts and bruises, Celia told them how afraid she and Gian had been that the search party would go down the other river instead of coming this way.

"We would have, but when we searched for signs at the crossing we found this," said Tormin holding up her rosary. As she looked at it gleaming in the firelight, two images filled her mind: one was of a face convulsed with hatred at the sight of the crucifix, and the other, of a great Shepherd rejoicing as He brought home His lost sheep. Yes, love could always bring good out of even the most terrible of hatreds.

Still later, after a Koinian had come back with the news that Gian had been found and would be brought over in the morning, Celia lay wrapped in a blanket while Dara and Tormin sat on each side of her singing softly. Their song sounded like an immense lullaby, full of their love of God, of each other, and of her. When it ended, she opened her eyes and saw both of them looking down at her and smiling. Then the old Celia from the shore of Lake Michigan, U.S.A., sleepily spoke for the last time, "I wonder why the Lord God ever dumped someone like me on you." And the new Celia of Koinia added even more sleepily, "Blessed is He."